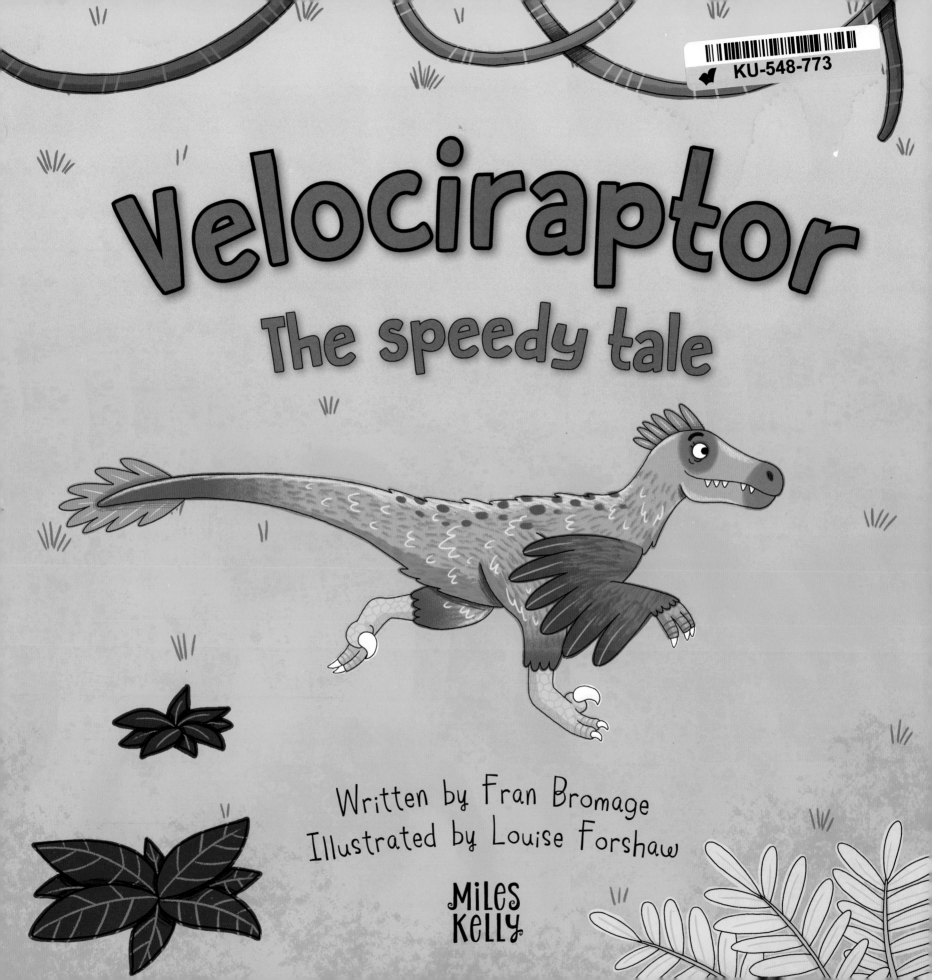

Velociraptor
The speedy tale

Written by Fran Bromage
Illustrated by Louise Forshaw

MILES
KELLY

Millions of years ago, there lived a Velociraptor called Vicky.

Vicky was **super-speedy.**
Everywhere she went,
she went in a rush.

"Got to go! **Can't stop!**"
she'd shout, ignoring her
baby brothers and sisters.

Vicky never **stopped to listen** or help her family.

While everyone else planned the next meal, Vicky **raced** around them.

"We'll follow the
Protoceratops herd tonight,"
said an old Velociraptor.

"We'll leave at... Vicky! Listen!"
But Vicky was off again.

When Vicky's family was **ready to hunt**, no one could find her.

"I'll see if I can **catch her**," said Vicky's friend, Gal.

Gal, a Gallimimus, was the only dinosaur **fast enough** to keep up with Vicky.

"Vicky!" called Gal when he spotted her. "Your family is..." But Vicky was off again.

Much later, Vicky finally **slowed down.**

She looked around her. The forest was **empty.** "Where is everyone?" Vicky said out loud.

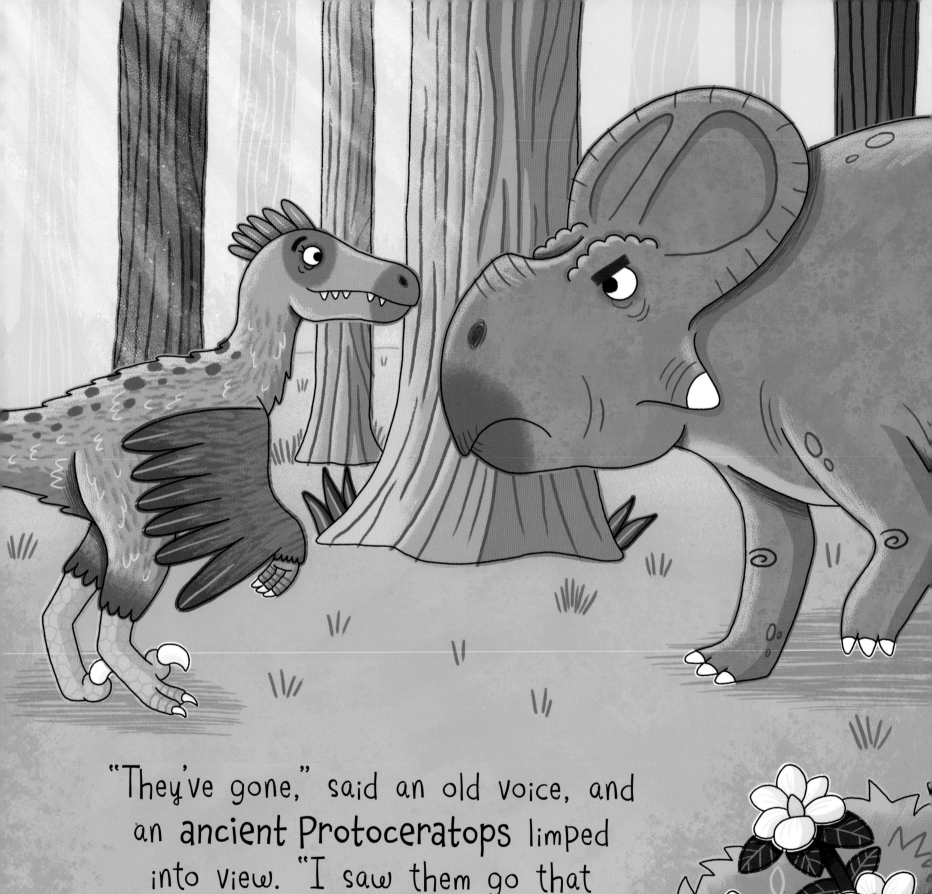

"They've gone," said an old voice, and an **ancient Protoceratops** limped into view. "I saw them go that way..." And Vicky was off again.

"You won't be eating any of my family tonight," **chuckled** the Protoceratops, peering down at Vicky.

As the old dinosaur ambled away, Gal tried to calm Vicky down.

"Stop flapping!" he shouted over the cliff.

"Slow down and use your claws," suggested Gal.

Another piece of the cliff broke away as Gal encouraged Vicky to keep climbing... slowly.

But once at the top, Vicky sped off again. "I saw my family! I need to go!" she told Gal.

"There's a shortcut through here," she yelled, and Vicky ran...

...straight into two huge Tarbosaurus!

"Aaaaah!" shrieked Vicky, turning around and racing the other way.

But as she headed deeper into the jungle, Vicky **raced into trouble** again!

The vines and creepers quickly trapped her.

"Stop rushing!" said Gal, when he finally found her. "You're running into trouble at every turn."

Gal helped Vicky **escape** and led her to a hiding place near the slimy swamp.

"We'll trap the Tarbosaurus in the swamp," said Gal. "Keep **shouting** so they come closer."

"Why?" asked Vicky. "We could just run."

"But we don't want to lead those two pea-brains straight to your family," replied Gal.

Both Tarbosaurus were soon **totally tied up** and stuck in the swamp.

A few moments later, Vicky and Gal emerged from the jungle.

They saw Vicky's family up on the hill. She was **excited** to see them again.

"Quietly and slowly," said Gal, "or we'll scare away the Protoceratops."

Vicky felt so grateful that Gal had taken the time to help her.

"Being fast is fun," she told the baby Velociraptors.

"But it's important to slow down, so you don't run into trouble."